Three Little Kittens

Lorianne Siomades

Boyds Mills Press

Published by Caroline House
Boyds Mills Press, Inc.
A Highlights Company
815 Church Street
Honesdale, Pennsylvania 18431
Printed in Hong Kong

Publisher Cataloging-in-Publication Data

Siomades, Lorianne.
Three little kittens / Retold and illustrated by Lorianne
Siomades. 1st ed.
[32]p. : col. ill. ;   cm.
Summary: A picture book based on the Mother Goose rhyme.
ISBN 1-56397-845-8
1. Nursery rhymes. 2. Children's poetry. [1. Nursery rhymes.
2.Poetry.]   I. Title.
[E]--dc21   2000   AC   CIP
99-63099

First edition, 2000
The text of this book is set in 36-point Times.

10 9 8 7 6 5 4 3

Three little kittens

They lost their mittens

And they began to cry . . .

"Oh, Mother dear, we sadly fear,
our mittens we have lost."

"What! Lost your mittens?
You naughty kittens.
Then you shall have no pie."

So the three little kittens,

They found their mittens,
And they began to cry . . .

"Oh, Mother dear, see here, see here,

Our mittens we have found!"

"What! Found your mittens?

Then you're good kittens!"

"Now where, oh where, is the pie?"